Four Little Teletubbies
A Finger Puppet Book

One day in Teletubbyland, Tinky Winky and Po were sitting on a hill.

You can join in the game with your Tinky Winky and Po finger puppets.

Two little Teletubbies sitting on a hill.

One named
Tinky Winky.

Eh-oh!

Eh-oh!

One named Po.

Run away
Tinky Winky!

Run away Po!

Come back
Tinky Winky!

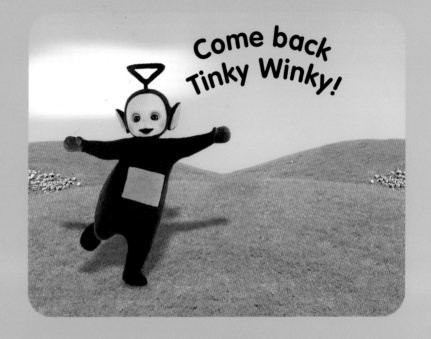

Come back Po!

Tinky Winky and Po love playing
Two Little Teletubbies.
They want to play it again and again!

You can play the game again with
Tinky Winky and Po.

One day in Teletubbyland, Laa-Laa and Dipsy were eating tubby toast.

You can join in the game with your Laa-Laa and Dipsy finger puppets.

Two little Teletubbies eating tubby toast.

Eh-oh!

One named
Laa-Laa.

Eh-oh!

One named
Dipsy.

Run away
Laa-Laa!

Run away
Dipsy!

Come back
Laa-Laa!

Come back
Dipsy!

Laa-Laa and Dipsy love playing
Two Little Teletubbies.
They want to play it again and again!

You can play the game again with
Laa-Laa and Dipsy.

All the Teletubbies love playing
Two Little Teletubbies.
And they love each other very much.

Big Hug!